Jan Has a Doll

Jan Has a Doll

Janice Earl

Illustrated by Tricia Tusa

Green Light Readers
Harcourt, Inc.
Orlando Austin New York San Diego Toronto London

Is that for Jan?

Where is Jan?
Go call Jan.

Where is Jan?

Look in here.
Look on the wall.

Is that for me?

It looks like me.

Now we can play!

Make Your Own Doll!

Jan's doll was made out of a corncob.
Can you create a doll of your own?

WHAT YOU'LL NEED

 **a cardboard tube
or rolled-up
paper**

 **collage
materials**

 tape

 **construction
paper**

 glue

 **markers or
crayons**

1. Use the tube for the doll's body. Draw a face on the tube.

2. Add arms and legs to the doll's body.

3. Use the construction paper and collage materials to dress and decorate your doll.

Now you have a doll just like Jan's!

Make a Friend

It's fun to make a new friend!

WHAT YOU'LL NEED

paper plate

yarn

crayons or markers

Popsicle sticks

pasta

tape

1. Make a paper plate puppet that looks like your new friend.

2. Have your friend make a puppet that looks like you.

3. When you're done, tape a Popsicle stick to the back of each puppet.

Then you can:

- Let your puppets do the talking.
  Use the puppets to tell stories about you and your new friend.

- Have a puppet show.
  Act out a way to be a good friend.

Meet the Illustrator

Tricia Tusa had lots of dolls when she was a little girl, but one of her favorites was a long, skinny doll made of cotton called Amelia. When Tricia saw Amelia in a shop, she asked her mother to buy the doll for her. But Tricia's mother said, "You have so many dolls. How about buying this one yourself, with the money you have saved from your allowance?" So Tricia did.

Now Amelia has been passed on to Tricia's eight-year-old daughter, who loves to play with her.

For information about permission to reproduce selections from this book, write to trade.permissions@hmhco.com or to Permissions, Houghton Mifflin Harcourt Publishing Company, 3 Park Avenue, 19th Floor, New York, New York 10016.

www .hmhco.com

First Green Light Readers edition 2005
Green Light Readers is a trademark of Harcourt, Inc., registered in the United States of America and/or other jurisdictions.

Library of Congress Cataloging-in-Publication Data
Earl, Janice.
Jan has a doll/Janice Earl; illustrated by Tricia Tusa.
p. cm.
"Green Light Readers."
Summary: Jan's father surprises her with a doll that looks like her.
[1. Dolls—Fiction.] I. Tusa, Tricia, ill. II. Title. III. Series: Green Light reader.
PZ7.E125Jan 2005
[E]—dc22   2004021930
ISBN 0-15-205168-6
ISBN 0-15-205167-8 (pb)

SCP 15 14 13 12 11
4500588253

Ages 4–6
Grades: K–1
Guided Reading Level: C–D
Reading Recovery Level: 5

Green Light Readers
For the reader who's ready to GO!

"A must-have for any family with a beginning reader."—*Boston Sunday Herald*

"You can't go wrong with adding several copies of these terrific books to your beginning-to-read collection."—*School Library Journal*

"A winner for the beginner."—*Booklist*

Five Tips to Help Your Child Become a Great Reader

1. Get involved. Reading aloud to and with your child is just as important as encouraging your child to read independently.

2. Be curious. Ask questions about what your child is reading.

3. Make reading fun. Allow your child to pick books on subjects that interest her or him.

4. Words are everywhere—not just in books. Practice reading signs, packages, and cereal boxes with your child.

5. Set a good example. Make sure your child sees YOU reading.

Why Green Light Readers Is the Best Series for Your New Reader

- Created exclusively for beginning readers by some of the biggest and brightest names in children's books

- Reinforces the reading skills your child is learning in school

- Encourages children to read—and finish—books by themselves

- Offers extra enrichment through fun, age-appropriate activities unique to each story

- Incorporates characteristics of the Reading Recovery program used by educators

- Developed with Harcourt School Publishers and credentialed educational consultants